Cinderella

STERLING CHILDREN'S BOOKS
New York

TEXT ADAPTATION GIADA FRANCIA

GRAPHIC DESIGN MARINELLA DEBERNARDI

FROM A FAIRY TALE BY
Charles Perrault

ILLUSTRATIONS BY
Francesca Rossi

A long time ago, in a great house, there lived two people who were very much in love. They had a beautiful little girl, and it seemed that nothing could threaten their happiness.

The father was a trader in precious fabrics and often traveled to distant and exotic lands. He described his journeys in the frequent letters he wrote home, which his wife and child loved to read. When a new letter arrived, the girl would run to sit next to her mother's favorite armchair, ready to hear about her father's adventures.

One terrible day, while the mother was opening a new letter, she suddenly clutched at her chest with her hand.

"Mother, what's wrong?" asked the concerned daughter.

"Nothing, little one. It's nothing. Don't worry."

But very soon it became clear that her mother's illness was very serious. When her father returned home, the doctors gave him the news that there was no hope of saving her.

When that sad winter had passed, spring returned and the time came for the father to leave once more. He knew that a long voyage lay before him and that he would be away for months, perhaps years. Fearing that his daughter would be very lonely, he married again. Even though he knew that no one could take the place of his first wife, he wanted to give the little one a mother.

His new wife already had two daughters of about the same age as his. The merchant hoped that the two stepsisters would become companions to his daughter, keeping her company and perhaps easing her sadness.

He did not know that the stepmother would soon reveal herself to be selfish and mean. He did not know that the two stepsisters, vain and cruel like their mother, would make his daughter's life miserable. Certainly, no one could have imagined such a change the day they arrived at their new home. They were all smiles when they got down from their carriage. The new mother and her daughters were greeted joyfully by the young girl. First, she showed her stepsisters their room, and then she showed them her toys.

Reassured, the merchant began to prepare for his departure.

"Girls, as soon as I reach port, I will send each of you a gift," he promised. "What would you like?"

"A new dress," cried one of the two stepsisters.

"And a china doll!" cried the other.

"I want two! And a doll's house. And new shoes!"

"So many requests!" The merchant smiled. "And you, my little one? What about you?"

"Father, I would like a tree."

"A tree?" he asked in surprise. The stepsisters burst out laughing.

"Yes, one of those trees you wrote about in your letters. Its branches full of white flowers that fall in the wind like drops of rain. I would like to plant one where my mother lies."

"An almond tree." Her father was moved. "Yes, my child, I will send you an almond tree."

He blew the girls a last kiss, mounted his horse, and galloped off.

Sadly, from that moment the young girl's life changed. The merchant's new wife could not bear the girl's beauty and gentleness. They were qualities that made her own daughters seem more vain and silly, and thus revealed their true nature.

The morning after the merchant's departure, she went into the girl's bedroom and pulled open the curtains.

"What's happening?" asked the sleepy child, sitting up and rubbing her eyes.

"From now on there will be some small changes," explained her stepmother, as the two stepsisters came in. They opened the wardrobe and started to pull out all her dresses.

"This room is larger than the one my daughters have. We can't have that. And you won't be needing so many dresses and toys."

"Why?" the little one asked, upset.

"Didn't I tell you? I had to let the cook and the maid go. You will do all the cooking and the housework for us."

"Me? But I—"

"Oh, don't mutter! I can't bear muttering! Do you want to stay in this house or not?"

"Of course. This is my home," whispered the child.

"Very well, get to work! You can start right away. There's breakfast to make."

"Yes, and do it quickly, because I'm starving!" said one of the stepsisters rudely.

"I'll just have tea, but I want it good and hot and with plenty of sugar," added the second, starting to pull out all the toys from the toy box.

"For breakfast I like cookies. And while you have the oven alight, don't forget to make the bread for lunch," concluded the stepmother. "Now go!"

The girl got up and ran to the kitchen, weeping. She hid under the table and stayed there all morning, her hands over her ears so that she could not hear her stepmother and stepsisters laughing. She knew that they were laughing at her. She missed her father and mother, and the life they once had.

For a moment, she thought of running away, but she quickly realized that she had nowhere to go. She could not even write to her father, because she had no idea where to send the letter. The only thing she could do was to wait for his return. The girl dried her tears and came out of her hiding place. She had decided to wait for her father bravely and with a smile.

From that day on, she worked hard from morning until night. She was forced to get up before dawn. She carried water from the well, lit the fire, cooked, and did the laundry.

At the same time, her stepsisters did all they could to humiliate and hurt her. They teased her and gave her hurtful nicknames. They saw that in the evenings, after she had finished tidying the kitchen, the girl would often fall asleep by the fire among the cinders. They started to call her "Cinderella."

The house constantly rang with their cruel laughter and the most absurd demands.

"Cinderella, bring me the hazelnut cookies, right away! But remember I don't like hazelnuts, so pick them all out!" said one.

"Today I can't seem to comb my hair. Come here, Cinderella! I want ringlets—but don't you dare curl my hair or you'll regret it!" added the other.

And so it went on for many months. Then one day a cart laden with boxes and parcels arrived in the courtyard. They were the presents that Cinderella's father had promised to his daughter and her stepsisters. All the toys and new clothes that he had sent to his own child were taken straight to the stepsisters' room, until the only thing that remained in the courtyard was the one thing she had asked for: the little almond tree. With it came a letter in which her father said that he must postpone his return. Cinderella read it with tears in her eyes. She took the almond tree and went to plant it in the place where she took refuge whenever she felt sad: the clearing where her mother lay.

Time passed very slowly. Season after season, year after year, Cinderella grew and became a splendid young woman. The almond tree grew, too. In spring it flooded the clearing with white petals, just as Cinderella had always imagined.

One morning, a strong breeze carried one of its flowers as far as the main courtyard of the royal palace. It dropped right onto His Majesty's royal crown as he watched his son's fencing lesson.

The king watched the young prince get the better of his fencing master with skill and confidence. He turned to the grand duke sitting next to him and said, "I think the time has come for my son to find a wife. He must learn that he has royal duties toward his subjects. I would like you to inform him."

"Your Majesty, he won't be very pleased with that! The prince has just returned after years traveling. He doesn't know any young women. Forcing him to marry someone he doesn't know could be difficult. You know as well as I do how rebellious His Highness can be."

"You're right! But still, I think the time is right. When I was his age . . ."

"What did you do?" asked the prince, amused. He threw down his sword and approached the pair.

"I was already king, and happily married to your mother. It's time you followed my example!"

"I don't know a single girl in the kingdom I could possibly marry."

"But this we can easily remedy," the grand duke quickly interjected. "We could invite every girl in the kingdom to the grand ball that we throw every year to celebrate spring."

"That's a wonderful idea," said the king. "Start arranging the invitations today. My son, I'm sure that one of these young women will steal your heart. I promise you that you will be free to marry whichever one you desire!"

"Then I hope that my soul mate's invitation doesn't get lost in the mail," the prince remarked sarcastically.

The invitations were sent out that same day:

Your worships are invited to the grand spring ball, which will take place on three consecutive evenings in the grand salon of the royal palace, in the presence of the king, the queen, and the prince, and at which, by order of His Majesty, every young woman in the kingdom shall be present.

Later that evening a valet appeared at Cinderella's house, right in the middle of an argument between the two stepsisters.

"Stop!" their mother silenced them. "Can't you see we have a guest? The king's messenger is here. We are invited to the palace for the spring ball. The prince is to choose his future wife from among the young women of the kingdom."

"An invitation to the palace!" shrieked the stepsisters in unison. The noise attracted Cinderella's attention, so she went to find out what was happening.

"Do you know what this means, my daughters? The time has come for the heir to the throne to get married. I'll bet that one of my daughters will be chosen by the prince," the stepmother said confidently.

"It will be me!" said one of the sisters.

"Not after he sees me!" exclaimed the other.

"Cinderella! Why are you standing there? Press our gowns and help the girls dress and do their hair!"

"I . . . well, I was thinking that—"

"How many times have I told you not to mutter! You know how much it annoys me!"

At these words Cinderella held up her chin, looked her stepmother in the face, and said in a loud voice, "The invitation says that all the young women in the kingdom are invited. I would like to go, too."

Everything went quiet. The two stepsisters and the stepmother stared at Cinderella for several seconds. Then they laughed.

"You? You, covered in cinders and muck! *You* want to go to the ball? You don't even have a pair of shoes to dance in!" cried her stepsister.

"Now stop being silly, Cinderella! Help the girls to get ready!" added the stepmother, glaring at her.

"While we're at the ball you can do the dusting. And be careful not to break anything, for once."

Ignoring her stepmother's protests, Cinderella ran from the house and headed for the almond tree without stopping.

As she was sobbing at the foot of the tree, she heard the rustling of wings. The girl dried her eyes and looked up into the branches of the tree. She saw a flock of doves, one of which had feathers as white as snow and seemed to be regarding her intently.

"Oh, how I long to be free like you," said Cinderella, lowering her gaze sadly. "And take flight for wherever I wish."

"And where would you go, my dear?" said a voice above her head.

"I would like very much to go to the ball and . . . wait! Who spoke?" asked Cinderella.

"Don't be afraid, I will do you no harm," said the white dove to the astonished girl. Then, with a gentle flutter of wings, the bird turned into a lady with the sweetest of faces.

"Who are you?"

"I am a flower fairy. I live in the branches of this almond tree, which your father sent from distant shores, and in which there is still magic. For years, I have watched you hide here looking for comfort, and I always hoped something would happen to restore your smile. But seeing that nothing has happened, I think it's time I helped."

The fairy smiled. "I would like to see you happy this evening, child. Tell me, what would you like? To go to the ball?"

"Yes, but I can't. I have only rags to wear, I don't know how to get to the palace, and my stepmother might recognize me!"

"No one will recognize you. Foolish people judge only by appearances. Sadly, your stepmother is no exception. When she sees the lady you are about to become, she will see only a young noblewoman. She will never see any similarity to the stepdaughter she left at home to do the cleaning. Now let's get to work! Bring me a pumpkin."

"I'll run and get one from the vegetable garden," said Cinderella. She had no idea how a pumpkin might help her go to the ball, but she followed the fairy's orders anyway. Picking the largest pumpkin that she could find, she carried it back to the almond tree.

"Well done! Now let's try to make this vegetable more useful."

The fairy raised her hands and whispered some words that Cinderella did not understand. Right away the pumpkin started to grow and change until it had become an elegant carriage. Cinderella was at a loss for words. But the fairy had only just begun! A lizard asleep on a branch became a coachman, and two field mice were transformed into white horses.

"There! Now, Cinderella, are you ready?" asked the fairy.

"Oh, thank you. I can't wait to go to the ball . . . but am I to wear these tattered old things?" asked Cinderella.

"How careless of me! No, absolutely not."

The fairy took a handful of almond petals and swirled them in the air. When she said the magic words, the flowers transformed into the most beautiful dress the girl had ever seen. The fairy looked her over.

"Now you just need a pair of shoes," she said. On her word, a pair of glass slippers appeared on the girl's feet, sparkling like diamonds.

"You really look like a princess. But I must now tell you something important. All my work will vanish on the stroke of midnight. Don't be late! Now go and enjoy yourself."

When Cinderella made her entrance at the ball, everything went quiet. No one had ever seen such a beautiful young woman.

Every lady at the party soon realized that they could never compete with her. It took only a single glance for the prince to know that he wanted only her at his side that evening. He went up to Cinderella, introduced himself with a bow, and asked her to dance. Then he took her by the hand and danced with her all night. He wanted no other girl.

The pair danced all evening, but when Cinderella heard the great clock sound the first strokes of midnight, she remembered the fairy's words. Whispering her apologies, she let go of the prince's hand and explained that she had to leave. He offered to accompany her, but Cinderella was scared that he might discover her true identity. She ran into the garden and hid behind a large birdhouse.

There she waited until the prince had returned to the ball. In the meantime her gown vanished, and her elegant hairstyle changed back to the loose locks that tumbled down her back.

Cinderella walked past her carriage, which had changed back into a pumpkin, and made her way home. She danced and skipping along the road, far too happy and excited to walk.

When her stepmother and stepsisters came home, they found Cinderella in the kitchen. She was fast asleep next to the fireplace, with a slight smile on her lips.

The next day the festival continued.

Cinderella had to press new gowns for her stepsisters and help them to fix their hair into elaborate styles. But this time it did not bother her, because she was dreaming about the evening before.

When everyone had left for the ball, the young girl ran to the almond tree to find the fairy.

"What a beautiful smile, little one. I think you must have enjoyed yourself last night. Am I right?"

"It was marvelous! The palace shone with lights. It was decorated with thousands of flowers and colored ribbons. The orchestra played so merrily. And the prince! He is so charming!" finished Cinderella with a smile.

"So, you might like to go back to the ball this evening?"

"Oh, would it be possible?" asked Cinderella hopefully. "May I have that beautiful gown?"

"I can give you one that is even more beautiful!" laughed the fairy. Then she took a handful of flowers from the tree and transformed them with her magic words.

The petals turned into a beautiful gold necklace, which adorned the sparkling gown that had also appeared. Cinderella put on the dress and instantly the glass slippers appeared on her feet.

That evening a dragonfly was transformed into a coachman, and two squirrels took the form of magnificent horses.

When the carriage arrived at the palace, the ball had already begun. The prince was bowing to the two-hundred-and-tenth and two-hundred-and-eleventh young ladies with an air of boredom. Suddenly he looked up and caught sight of Cinderella at the entrance. As if in a trance, he abandoned the other girls and went toward her. He took her by the hand and accompanied her to the grand salon, where he did not let her go the entire evening.

Again, the hours flew by, and all too soon the twelve strokes of midnight rang throughout the palace. Cinderella knew that the magic was about to come to an end.

This time, the girl said good-bye with just a brief curtsy, leaving the prince right in the middle of a dance.

Cinderella reached the carriage at a run, and was climbing in when the prince ran out of the palace looking for her. When he saw her leaving, he jumped on a horse and started to follow her. But after the first bend in the road, the carriage disappeared without trace. All that the prince found was a large pumpkin and two little squirrels who were heading for the woods.

Moments later, he was joined by a knight.

"Your Highness, is everything all right? We saw you leave at a gallop. Is something wrong?"

"Yes, my friend. I have lost the woman of my dreams. One moment she was in my arms, and the next she had disappeared, carriage and all."

Hidden among the branches of a tree that she had just managed to scramble up before the prince arrived, Cinderella listened to this conversation.

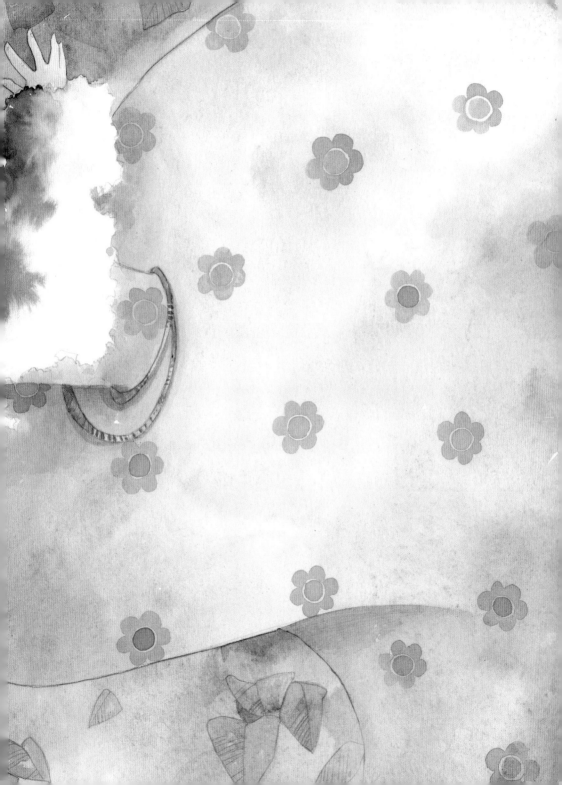

When the young man mounted his horse and rode away, Cinderella climbed down from the tree feeling very sad. She was happy that she had been able to go to the ball for a second time and to have seen the prince again, but leaving him had been very difficult.

Cinderella trembled to think that she had risked revealing her secret. All night she wondered whether to go back to the almond tree to ask again for the fairy's help, or to resign herself to her real life. But when the next evening arrived, her desire to see the prince was too strong. The fairy assisted her for a third time. She created out of thin air, with a slight movement of her fingers, the most sumptuous ball gown that Cinderella had yet worn.

When Cinderella entered the palace for the third time, all the guests turned to look at her. They whispered to one another, wondering who this mysterious girl was who had stolen the prince's heart. The prince looked at her with an expression that made the old king very happy. His son had finally found the bride of his dreams.

The orchestra began to play, but the prince did not want to dance. He wanted to find out more about this mysterious girl. He had not stopped thinking about her for two days.

"Where do you come from?" he asked her.

"I have always lived in your kingdom, Your Highness."

"But you have never come to the palace, have you? Are you from a noble family?"

"What makes a person noble? If it's only a title determined by one's birth, then, no. I am not."

"Don't you have a name?"

"Yes, Your Highness, we all have a name."

"But you don't want to tell me yours, do you?"

"No, not now. Please, let's not spoil this marvelous music with words. Let us have this dance."

The prince did as she asked, and Cinderella was so happy that she almost missed the clock striking midnight. Only on the last stroke did she realize that her gown was starting to change. Frightened, she cried, "I have to go!"

"Don't go, wait! I don't know your name or where to find you!"

But Cinderella slid her hand out of the prince's, then ran through the palace and down the grand staircase. She lost one of her glass slippers, but did not stop, scared that someone would catch up with her.

The prince raced out of the grand salon, but he stopped when he saw the slipper that had been left behind. He picked it up and held it close.

"I know you're out there somewhere," he said to himself. "And when I find you, you will become my queen."

When the sisters returned from the ball, Cinderella asked them if they had enjoyed themselves. They said that a mysterious lady had fled the ball in such a hurry that she lost one of her glass slippers. The prince had picked it up, and for the rest of the night had done nothing but stare at it.

A few days later the king's son issued a proclamation throughout the land. He would marry the woman whose foot fitted the shoe perfectly. Valets were sent to the homes of all the girls in the kingdom, and one arrived at Cinderella's house that morning. The stepmother ran to wake her lazy daughters.

"Do you have any other daughters, ma'am?" asked the valet.

"No!" she replied.

"So who is this young woman?" he asked, pointing to Cinderella. She was staring at the glass shoe from the top of the stairs.

"It's just our servant!" replied the stepmother, exasperated.

"My orders are to try the slipper on every girl in the kingdom."

Cinderella went up to him, ignoring the looks from her stepsisters. The valet offered her the shoe, and she tried it on . . .

The shoe fit!

"What?" cried the two stepsisters in unison.

"But it's not possible!" howled the stepmother. "This girl is just our servant! While we were at the ball, she was at home sweeping. It's not possible that she is the same person!"

Hearing this, the valet got up to leave. The girl was indeed beautiful, but she did not look like the mysterious lady who had come to the palace in a fancy carriage.

At that moment, the doves from the almond tree

flew in through the windows. The largest dove landed on Cinderella's outstretched hand. At its touch, the girl transformed. It was clear that she was the unknown beauty who had stolen the prince's heart.

The girl was immediately led to the royal palace, where at last she was able to tell the prince her name and explain everything that had happened.

One month later, amid great feasting and the ringing of all the bells in the kingdom, Cinderella married the prince. And they lived happily ever after.

STERLING CHILDREN'S BOOKS
New York

An Imprint of Sterling Publishing
387 Park Avenue South
New York, NY 10016

First Sterling edition 2015
First published in Italy in 2014 by De Agostini Libri S.p.A.

ISBN 978-1-4549-1508-9

Distributed in Canada by Sterling Publishing
c/o Canadian Manda Group, 165 Dufferin Street
Toronto, Ontario, Canada M6K 3H6
For information about custom editions, special sales, and
premium and corporate purchases,
please contact Sterling Special Sales at 800-805-5489 or
specialsales@sterlingpublishing.com.

Translation: Contextus s.r.l., Pavia, Italy (Louise Bostock)
Editor: Contextus s.r.l., Pavia, Italy (Martin Maguire)

Manufactured in China
Lot #:
2 4 6 8 10 9 7 5 3 1
11/14
www.sterlingpublishing.com/kids

—